Proper Dragon Tales No.1

The Black Mountain Sheep

Words and Pictures by Caroline Downey

Caroline Downey

D1318463

The artwork in this book is available as prints.

This book is dedicated to all those who believe in Dragons

An old saying explains that the Black Mountains enchant all who visit and, like a magnet, will always attract you back to return again and again, and even today this theme continues. Proper Dragon Tales are stories set in this magical area and are best read aloud on the side of a 'sheep scattered' Welsh mountain. Whilst every effort has been made to keep the authenticity of this story, the use of precise English grammar may have suffered in the translation from 'Proper Dragon' Speak. All the characters and events in this book are fictional, any resemblance to actual people or creatures living or dead is purely coincidental. The locations described intend to capture the essence of the Black Mountains countryside and are not an exact portrayal. The author cannot be responsible for anyone getting lost or injured whilst attempting to find these places.

NB In 2001 the 'Foot and Mouth' disease was highlighted in parts of the U.K. The government imposed tight restrictions prohibiting movement of farm animals and access on grazing land to stop the infection spreading. All farm animals considered positive, including those occupying neighbouring land, were culled. Subsequently, all the sheep grazing on the open land of the Black Mountains were collected and culled, although all tests later proved negative. They were replaced with new sheep when the restrictions were lifted.

I be the one who tells

From the beginning my place was to be found on the edge of Wales in the steep rocks of the Black Mountains. My home is a lovely, dark and smelly place that keeps the weather out. Nobody calls, not even a nosy owl. I pass the time of day forecasting the Welsh weather, sensing its shifting moods, as I keep guard over my lovely valley. I see streams tumble into rivers and leaves turn from green to gold, where carpets of bluebells burst through rusty bracken and forests hide dark secrets. Every now and again I go off exploring over my lovely patch. I watch over those furry creatures playing in the ferns and see them humble folk go back and fro to their stony dwellings. Though I do be careful – as of an evening when the sun is setting or the moon be full or when I pass under a rainbow – you may just spy my scaly shape. But I've no wish to be seen. By now I consider myself the keeper of these lovely Mountains and all those that be there and it's heaps of fun gazing over all them meagre and mighty matters.

I suppose I know of all those hidden happenings – if you care to listen I might just be the one who tells you a *Proper Dragon's Tale*........

So cwtch up and step into my pages.

1-2 My Lovely Valley

The Black Mountain Sheep

Darkness had fallen fast in the Valley. It was the longest night of the year. The stars shone brightly like poached eggs hovering high over this peculiar part of the Black Mountains. Yes, peculiar because dragons don't exist in any other places.

The isolation of this area makes it a grand place to live, where tumbledown dwellings and historic ruins are now reclaimed by nature. There was a full moon on this remarkable evening, highlighting features of this lovely valley. Trees recline at alarming angles and stone walls buckle and reshape themselves. The soft mossy ground fills the spaces between and warm hints of winter bracken patchwork the landscape. Heather crowns the barren mountain tops scored by criss-cross, sheep trodden, pathways where, on this eventful evening, two little lambs dared to stray from their grazing land.

The wintry bleakness is the finest time of the year. There is a hill shaped like a Christmas pudding that is broken and crumbling as if sliced in search of its treasure. The scaly formation of rocks on its steep side is like a giant dragon's tail. One might think this was the cause of the creeping landslide that distorts all beneath its pathway - its mighty weight squeezing the earth down the steep hillside and the creator of the crooked village below.

A strangely divine victim of this happening is the little crooked church, its moonlit tower slants dramatically, appearing in the darkness as a huge rocket ready for lift off. Surrounding the church a congregation of large headstones seem to sway gracefully in dreamy contemplation throwing angel-wing shadows within its wobbly walled churchyard. Dotted around the village are its leaning cottages that have wonky windows lit up like fairy lights, their attached sloping porches and tilting sheds depend on their support. In the gardens a hen house is braced with bricks, a kennel is propped with posts and an outside loo has its door bottom trimmed at an acute angle to ease its usage.

With my fine dragony sight I see Ginger Thomas waving his tail as he meanders down the pathway off to play with his pal Fluffy who grooms his fur to one side. The pony in the paddock seems to have two legs shorter on one side to cope with the slope. Roadways snake around large twisted trees, humps and bumps and rocky outcrops. Each rambling estate is enclosed by drifting boundaries, bending and blending into the warped scenery happily conforming to nature. There the humble folk wedge up their furniture tidy, learn to plaster up cracked walls and constantly straighten pictures. In the bar of the topsy-turvy tavern folded beer mats steady tables on the undulating flagstones where patrons feel tipsy before they are, in this peculiar part of the Black Mountains.

1-3 The Crooked Village

Further up the valley I can hear with my fine dragony ears Meg the sheepdog yapping, and find her keenly snapping at the tractor tyres as Farmer Jones drives the rusty wreck about the farmyard. The area is lit up by a bright outside light that glows in the shadowy hillside. The grubby white farmhouse has little windows with colourful curtains that shine out a cosy warmth. Indoors Mrs Jones, who is always found in a flowery apron, is busy in the kitchen. By the back door a huge oak tree stands guard over the mucky cobbled farmyard, its swaying limbs rattling on the wrinkly-tin roof of the barn.

The barn has corroded corrugated panels that flap and clatter in need of proper repair, instead deformed nails and baler twine crudely secure them in temporary restoration. Through a gap in the barn I can see the sheep marked with blue blots on their backs. Smelly, steamy heat radiates from their scruffy coats and hangs in the air as they huddle up close together. There was excitement amongst them after their busy day.

That morning I watched the flock being gathered up and guided down from the mountain to the shelter of the farm, for the Welsh weather had come early and snow could be smelt.

The sheep were now happily chewing on the hay that Farmer Jones had just cut open for them - all except for one miserable Mother Ewe.

The big barn doors clanked closed, Farmer Jones had finished his day's tasks and headed back to the farmhouse with Meg at his heels. I take my chance, with my fine nose, to have a gaze into the barn - being careful not to make dragon prints in the muddy yard. The sad sheep's fleecy friend struts up to her. "What is the maatter Baabara?" asks Wilmaa.

"I can't find my twins," she worriedly replies. "In fact I have not seen them aall daaay!" Her woolly topknot bobs about on her head as she frowns. Wilmaa reassures her, "Don`t worry, they are big laambs now, perhaps they have staayed up on the mountain."

Baabara gasped with horror. "But the snow is coming and it will be faar colder than we have ever known!" Wilmaa thought for a while "I will go and call for Meg the sheep dog, she might know where the laambs aare."

She pushes her way towards the gap in the barn. I quickly step back, as creatures can sense me, and whoops, make a dragon print in the mud. The two sheep can see Meg's wooden kennel across the yard and they wait anxiously for her to appear.

You may think at this stage, me being a clever old dragon, I'd have the magic to make it all better again - but I am a proper dragon that can only watch and wish that events do end properly — and besides, there be no proper story to be told without an adventure.

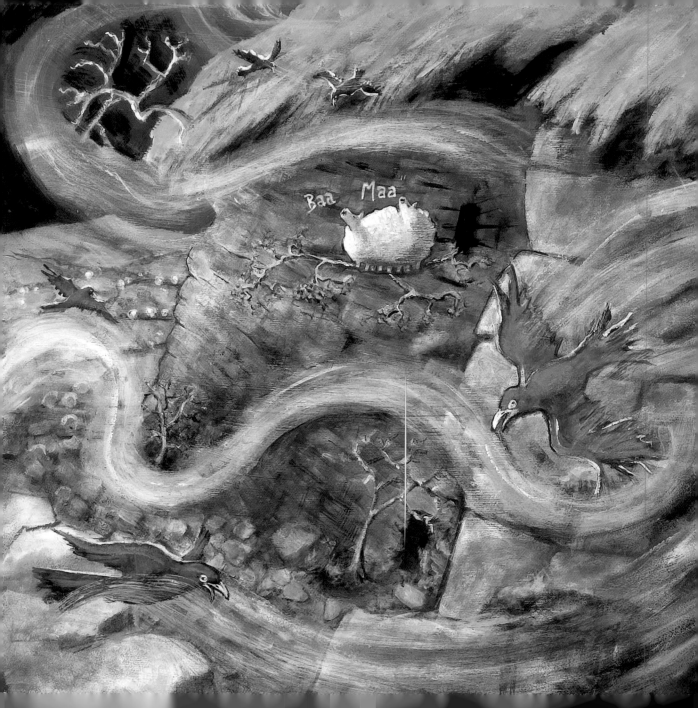

Above the farm the wind thundered along the ridge of the mountain like an express train roaring along its steely rails. On the steep rock face bare trees jut out from the rocks, each limb posing spookily with its fingers in readiness to catch tumbling boulders that dislodge from time to time. Over the centuries these massive rocks have fallen into the hidden gorge below to form an incredible landscape similar to an alien planet. The drizzling water from the cliff began to freeze and turned into icicles while frost was coating the ground.

Farmer Jones had brought his sheep home just in time – no creature would dare to exist on the mountain tonight. But up there, on the rocky side of the mountain, as the wind eased, a feeble sheepish cry could just be heard... "Baa-Maa. Baa-Maa." Then a mean dose of Welsh weather overwhelmed the bleats and hailstones scratched the rugged countryside.

I spied the two frightened lambs desperately balancing on an old twisted branch yielding shiny red berries. It was growing from the side of the mountain at a fearful height half-way down, or would that be half-way up? No-one heard these poor little lambs, all sensible creatures were tucked up snugly in their own little homes. No-one was out chancing the elements, except for the crafty crows flying above who chose to ignore them while playing 'plunge and peck' in the wind.

Why on earth did those lambs go there? You may well ask. I don't think they were studying the pretty rock lichen or finding the rare fronded fern. No, it was earlier in the day when the foolhardy twins Zak and Zoe had strayed off their patch. Their mother Baabara had not noticed her beloved twins had gone missing as they normally played with the other lambs while the flock watched over them. Unlike their old home ground, this one had no fences to keep them safely in.

Zak and Zoe had become bored with the taste of the fusty winter grass and had wandered to the edge of the mountain to find more tempting nibbles. Unflustered and full of youthful pluck the twins ventured carefully down the rocks to 'check out' that tree with the deliciously looking berries. Successfully reaching the branch they found themselves stranded unable to climb up or downward.

They were, as you might say left out on a limb. A pitiful sight as their thoughts turned to their Maa and flock. They longed to be back frolicking around on the mountain, dashing up the cairns and baaing at the top, and their very favourite lark was to chase after ramblers and flee when they turned to see them. Now they shivered alone in their shabby cream fleeces. "Baa-Maa, Baa-Maa!" the duet pathetically continued into the night while I pondered on how I could get them down safely.

Then for a fleeting spell all went quiet as a reply was heard.

"Whoot are you calling" was the response. The twins wobbled on their branch with amazement. Out of the darkness a big-eyed owl poked his head out of a crack in the rocks. It was my noisy neighbour Howell the Owl, not the most sympathetic creature when you are trying to sleep at night.

"What a hoot," he squawked in petty jollity as he saw the lambs occupying his perch; he wasn't used to company.

"Help us, we are stuck on this branch," exclaimed Zak.

"That's very interesting," said the Owl. "Especially as it's not a gum tree," and he annoyingly laughed in his Welsh tone.

Zak and Zoe were not cheered by his silly comment and cwtched up closer, suspecting impending doom. An almighty streak of lightning, followed by an enormous clap of thunder filled the sky making the lambs wobble but not quite enough to fall off. Owl, unfazed at the weather, began to flap his wings proudly in order to capture the lambs' attention, "So you are the English sheep – we've never had foreign flocks up here before." He extended his neck to look at them closely. The lambs appeared to Howell as one big ball of wool on twiggy legs. This comical sight made Owl hoot with laughter until a peculiarly huge blast of wind blew the lot of them down the side of the mountain – Was that wishful thinking? Oh well, it got them off the branch.

The lambs went tumbling, spinning, spluttering and fluttering downwards as gravity plunged them into the bleak dismal space below.   Zak and Zoe's lives flashed before them — they see a blur of green grass with a dash of daisy, until THUD! They bounced and bounced again cushioned by their woolly coats, while Owl followed flapping his wings as he spun a cartwheel 'head over claws' until he landed in a heap beside them. All around was the amazing sight of the big fallen rocks that had come to rest in the gully, near the start of the farm fields.

After picking themselves up the lambs saw Owl with his feathers tangled up in a heap and took their chance to mock him, "Is that how Welsh owls fly? haa, baa." The crows above joined in and squawked, "haw-haw....haw-haw!" Howell ignored them and brushed himself smart with his wings then in justification explained, "There is nothing more fierce than the Wooelsh wooeather." He flew up above the lambs and beckoned them to follow him along the moonlit terrain.

Zak and Zoe carefully jumped from boulder to boulder trying not to slip or do the splits on the slippery stones. Howell hoots to hurry them up as he sees the storm advancing from up the valley. Soon they reach a craggy hole in the rocks, the entrance to a dreary looking cave and Howell quickly flew off to the shelter of his home.

The lambs felt very worried for they needed their mother to keep them warm and safe and had forgotten to ask the Owl if he had seen her. They were abandoned in this strange place and now confronted with the challenge of entering the dreaded cave that loomed before them. How they wished they had never left the safety of the flock.

The ground was beginning to freeze and Zak and Zoe realised a night outside in the cold would be far more daunting. They leaned against each other for courage and began to step into the black hole. Suddenly from behind a boulder up popped the bossy bunny known as Bobbin.

"Stop dithering and get in!" he demanded and impatiently pointed his paw towards the cave.

Startled by the unexpected order the lambs scampered into the dark and creepy chamber where the dripping of running water echoed around and the smell of something strange lurked amid. Zak whispered to Zoe, "Did I imagine an evil glint in that rabbit's eyes?" as he questioned Bobbin's motive to get them into the cave. Soon they felt warmer as the chilly Welsh weather failed to reach them. Reluctantly they settled down on the pebbly ground tucking their dainty legs beneath them and soon the tired lambs fell asleep. They were now safe and warm and I slip away leaving them snoring their little woolly heads off.

Snow silently fell in the night and whitened the landscape. Back at the farm, because of the coldness, Meg was allowed to sleep by the welly boots in the utility room. The scent of her master's stinky damp jacket and coats made her imagine that she was in doggy heaven and had sweet, smelly dreams. Meg is a young dog, she was the runt of the litter, and came from a farm further up the valley. Her father was meant to be a champion sheepdog but lately Farmer Jones doubted this claim because Meg would rather play about than listen to his commands. Meg slept well until Merlin the Cat sneaked in with a mouse and chased it around the room. The cockerel crowed as usual at the crack of dawn – morning had arrived.

The sheep in the barn stirred, Wilmaa and Baabara had stayed all night at that draughty gap in the barn waiting for Meg to appear. They had watched in turn until the outside light flashed on and the farmhouse door opened. Out rushed Meg excited to see the snow, she skipped and danced, biting at the fluffy settlement. Merlin leaped on to the roof of Meg's kennel in fear of a playful nip.

The two ewes bleated loudly trying so hard to gain Meg's attention. Soon the other sheep joined in, oblivious of their purpose until they all called together making a real racket. "Baa-Meeg, baa-Meeg!" Even the farmer's wife pulled back the kitchen curtain to see what the fuss was about.

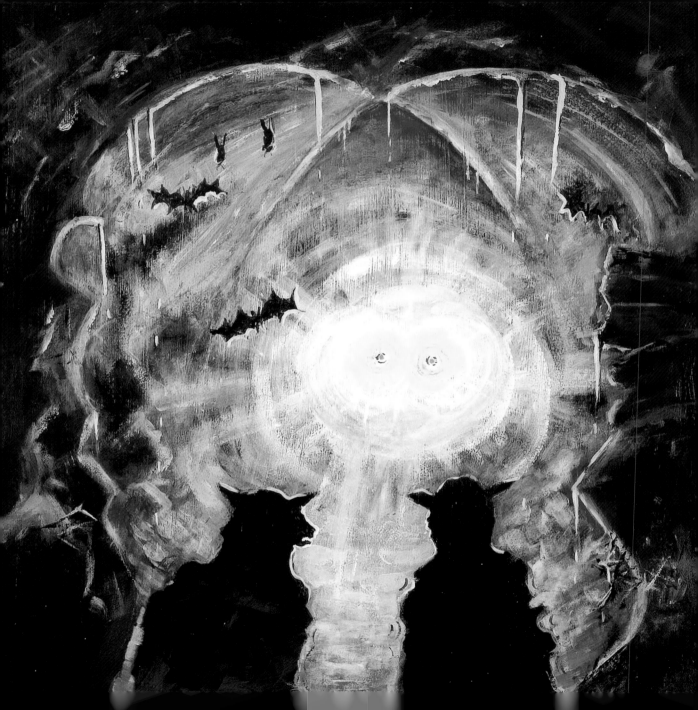

In the morning the cave was still dark as Welsh coal. Zoe woke first with a feeling of impending danger as she quietly woke Zak. There was something stirring in the depth of the tunnel, scuffle, shuffle, huff and puff. A heavy, stinky, gassy stench filled the atmosphere as the 'thing' approached, the lambs trembled on the spot.

Then Zak knew, the rabbit had tricked them into entering the cave and this must be the big cat of the Black Mountains! A young lamb or two for breakfast would keep a panther full up for days. The smell became stronger as the beast crept closer. Out of the darkness appeared two huge, veiny, green eyes, they shone like torches that pulsated and lit up the cave.

It groaned then growled at Zak and Zoe in the deepest vibration an ear could detect. "Saeson gwynion." A most spooky sound thought the lambs as they slowly stepped backwards, stumbling on pebbles as they pondered on what it was saying. Again, "Saeson gwynion." Its eyes dilating to focus on its victims as it draw nearer to the lambs. They soon found their bottoms firmly pressed against the cave wall and had nowhere else to go. Around them bats bombed about the spitting stalactites dangling from the rugged rocky roof.

To a dragon the cave is like a magnificent gothic cathedral but to Zak and Zoe it was a grim place to end their days. Horror-struck, the lambs shook so much their fleeces seemed to uncurl.

"Act dead." Zak panicked, "It won't attack if we are still."

"Do you want me to find the mint sauce!" retorted Zoe, unwilling to sacrifice herself without a fight. But Zak pulled her down and they surrendered themselves with eight legs awkwardly sticking upwards.

"English whites!" Came the growl again. "Well, more like the colour of a lost old handkerchief," it added in a tuneful lilt that confused the lambs more. Its bulging eyes flickered and its breath stank of old walking boots. Zak felt his nose twitch from the bad smell. He buried his face into Zoe's fleece, but he couldn't stop his nose from tickling and violently blew out an enormous sneeze. "Baa-chooo!" Wool and nose-sniff exploded everywhere and the beast backed away in disgust.

The lambs jumped to their feet as they sensed the creature strutting pass them towards the entrance to the cave. Zak and Zoe followed curiously until a shaft of dazzling brightness enveloped them. For a weird moment they thought they had been eaten and were on their way to heaven. They blinked and squinted until their eyes got used to the light – there before them was the menacing silhouette of the beast. They struggled to distinguish the creature's identity. Its copper-coloured form had prickly brambles trailing from its bulky belly and it swaggered along on bandy legs. Then to their relief they recognized it as an old tatty sheep.

Turning to the lambs she revealed, "I am Ewa, the last of Black Mountain Sheep and I suppose you are the new kids on the Black?" She looked at them with a disapproving motherly look and tuts, "You'll be hungry," and she led them to a clump of grass near the entrance of the cave. Zak and Zoe looked in wonder at the cold white stuff on the ground.

"That is snow," said Ewa and inquires, "you two should be down on the farm by now, its always two coats colder up here."

"Is that where our flock is?" asked Zoe and then realised why their Maa did not hear them.

"Why aren't you down on the faarm with them?" Zak quizzed Ewa, exposing his green tongue as he munched away on a mouthful of grass.

"I never go down," she explained proudly. "I am from the original Black Mountain sheep. It makes us special. The mountain is harsh and rugged without fences but by instinct we sheep know our own boundary and will not stray. This sense will be passed on to our lambs but if they choose to go down in the winter to the farm they will return in the spring to their own patch of mountain. We are the colour of bracken when it changes in winter, just like it is now. The redder we are the more tough and fiery our nature. Over many generations we had become a hardy breed with a strong spirit."

"Where are the rest of your flock now?" asks Zoe.

"It is a tragic tale," bleated Ewa, "But it has to be told."

The twins knelt down against each other and listened solemnly.

"It was a while ago, the flock had been gathered in for winter. Only the bold ones stayed and sheltered by the rocks. We remained the landladies of the mountain – just like our ancestors who grazed here over the centuries. Sam the ram stayed with us and we felt very safe. Then one evening we noticed a strange smell in the air. It had drifted from far away. We few became distressed, something seemed very wrong. Days later we heard muffled cries from our flock down in the valley. It was terrible and there was nothing we could do. No farmers walked the hills, no Meg-dog came to visit. Something awful must have happened.

Sometime later when we thought it had passed, I saw a humble-being, dressed all in white, coming our way. We scattered in fright when the shotgun blasts came around us. I ran down the rocks, falling and jumping until I found the shelter of this cave. I trembled for days. Then I called out, again and again, until my baa had gone. There was no reply, the others must have perished and the flock never returned."

Ewa turned her head as a tear rolled down her face. "So I am the last of the Black Mountain Sheep and I am old and will not last much longer." Zak and Zoe blinked back their tears.

Zoe whispered to Zak. "That must have been the dreaded Foot and Mouth disease - Maa had said she heard mutterings from the market."

Ewa bent her knees and rolled on her side. "I can't be coping with another winter, just leave me here," she puffed.

The twins jumped up and pleaded with her to get up, but she started panting and strained to keep her head off the cold ground. It began snowing again with big fuzzy flakes. Zak and Zoe watched as they gently floated down to rest on Ewa's big tangled tummy. This snow stuff was an unfamiliar sight, as the lambs had not seen anything like it before.

"I wish I knew what to do," said Zoe.

"Let's call for Howell," suggested Zak. So they both bleated as loudly as they could, calling baa-owl!

Bobbin popped up and told them to shut up but quickly disappeared as Howell the Owl swooped down and complained, "Don't you know it's daytime, I should be fast asleep."

"Look at Ewa," Zoe exclaimed.

Howell glided nearer to Ewa and wisely scrutinised the old girl.

"She doesn't look well," he hooted. "She will freeze out here if we can't get her into the cave."

But Ewa would not move from her place on the cold snow.

Back at the farm, Farmer Jones opened the barn door to find his sheep pacing about creating a right lot of noisy bleating. He wondered if the flock didn't like their new home or if the hay had upset their tummies? Baabara and Wilmaa took their chance to jostle their way through the flock and slip pass the puzzled farmer just as he was unfastening the hurdle gate, they rushed out into the yard. Then to his horror, Farmer Jones found the rest of the sheep followed at great pace, knocking him back as they trotted out on to the carpet of snow. Meg instinctively tried to round them up but the flock soon surrounded her.

"You must help us!" baaed Wilmaa. "Baabara can't find her laambs."

"I've never lost a woolly," barked Meg, offended. She could remember when those cheeky lambs had first arrived on the farm and they had teased her with their silly English words.

"Well they must have got themselves lost," Meg defended herself.

"So they are still on the mountain!" bawled Baabara.

The flock gasped in horror and began to chant, "You'aa fault, you'aa fault!"

"Orrite, orrite, I'll go and find them," snapped Meg. She knew it would be thick with snow up there but felt annoyed that she had failed to round up all her sheep and knew if word got out the other dogs wouldn't even give her half a sniff. Meg put her nose into the air and pointed it towards the hills.

Farmer Jones shouted at Meg to get the flock back into the barn as Mrs Jones rushed out of the farmhouse, still in her slippers. But Meg ignored him, barked and jumped the yard gate leading up the track to the mountain.

"Best go and get her," suggested Mrs Jones, "I'll finish off here."

Farmer Jones cursed under is breath, "Stupid dog, of all the days to run off she finds the worst day of the year." He had a good mind to leave her to make her own way home especially as Mrs Jones had the bacon and eggs on.

The blizzard was bitter up on the mountainside. Zoe started crying as she nuzzled up to Ewa, she urged her to get up but the old sheep was too weak.

"I'll go for help," announced Zak "I'll find my way somehow to the farm."

Howell shook the flakes off him and explained it would be too difficult in the snow – impossible to squeeze through the thick hedgerows, jump the high walls and all gates are shut tight – a sheep would never be able to make it.

"We must do something," begged Zoe.

Howell thought hard until he unwillingly announced, "It's morning, I am really tired – as it's way passed my bedtime, I'm hungry – as I haven't even caught a good supper and it is so bright that I can hardly see, but I suppose I'm the only one to doo wit, so I will doo wit, doo wit!"

The complaining Owl swivelled his head completely around until he found his direction.

Zak and Zoe watched hopefully as Howell flapped off and disappeared into the white of the snowflakes. He was cursing the weather as he struggled to see his way down to the farm – he was only used to flying in the dark. He followed the snowy ruts of the track from gate to gate across the fields that he knew would lead him to the farmyard.

After a while he got quite exhausted so stopped for a rest on one of the gates. He turned and looked back to the mountain, but he only saw a white barrier of falling snow. Then just as he was about to continue his journey, BASH! YELP! and FLUTTER! Howell was bumped off his perch sending feathers everywhere as he struggled to regain his balance. He went spinning and crashing.

"What in the skies was that?" he squawked.

Below him was a stunned Meg, she had not seen Howell as she jumped the gate and was now yelping in pain because she had twisted her leg. Poor Meg was unable to go on.

Zak and Zoe stayed close to Ewa. She continued to puff and pant but insisted that the lambs should go into the cave to keep warm. Both felt helpless but desperately wanted to help this poor sheep that had suffered so much. I felt sad to see this grand old lady in such distress. She was, as she had told, the last of her kind.

"Let's go to the edge and call for help," suggested Zak and they agreed it was better than doing nothing. So jumping along the big boulders and over a snowy bank they soon came to a narrow walled route that was tree lined with prickly hawthorn.

The branches drooped weirdly with the weight of the snow and this spooked the lambs. They stopped and bleated, "We're hereaa, we're hereaa!" but their calls were lost in the snowy storm. Eventually they tried to retrace their tracks – but the snow had covered them up. In a panic Zak and Zoe bounded about looking for clues but found themselves completely confused. The snow stuck to their fleecy coats until they looked like snowballs.

Then, to their horror, the snow slipped from beneath them sending the twins rolling down the hillside into bigger snowballs. Crashing to a halt, the snow crumbled off them, as they hit the hedgerow full of prickly briers. But what a mess, their tangled-up wool fastened to the dead brambles – a knitting disaster.

With great difficultly Zak and Zoe heaved themselves out from the hedgerow, extracting the brambles with them. Entwined and grumbling they scuffled along following the boundary until they came to a gate. It was secured shut with bailer twine and the two lambs could only poke their heads through the bars and moan pitifully.

Zak and Zoe were exhausted and cold and were giving up on ever being found when amazingly out of the white flew Howell, followed by Meg limping awkwardly. The lambs wriggled with glee to see them. Meg nuzzled her nose though the gate bars and was so relieved to find them safe and well, the flock will be happy again. Then her ears tingled and pricked up alertly, she whined anxiously as she could hear her master's rickety tractor chugging along.

Farmer Jones stopped at the gate, got out and ordered his dog into the cab. Meg appealingly held up her paw, so he carried her hastily to the box that was attached to the back of the tractor. He then went and opened the gate to let the lambs into the field. "Get in, you little rascals!" and he gave them his boot up their backsides. "My breakfast is getting cold," he cussed as he went to close the gate behind them.

The twins bleated. "You must find Ewa!" and jumped back up the track. Repeatedly they tried to get Farmer Jones to understand while they dodged his attempts to grab them. Meg, who was nursing her paw, understood and insisted too "Woof, woof let's find Ewa!" The farmer stood still in bewilderment. He scratched his brow, straightened his cap and reluctantly decided to continue up the snowy hill. Howell led the way while Zak and Zoe squashed themselves into the box with Meg. They prayed that Ewa would be found alive.

The tractor slipped along the rutty trail until they reached the spooky tree-lined track, Farmer Jones switched on the lights to see his way through. The low spiky branches scratched the tractor as it passed by.

Bobbin the Bunny watched from the foot of the mountain as the tractor progressed. When it got nearer he scampered away, frightened of the bright tractor lights, aware that rabbit and headlamps is a bunny's worst nightmare.

The tractor bumped to a stop at the edge of the big boulders. Zak and Zoe jumped out into the soft deep snow that reached up to their tummies. Meg was determined to come too and carefully followed them, hopping on three legs, into the hoof-prints of the lambs. Farmer Jones trudged along and soon his muddy boots became clean – he still wasn't sure why he was needed but followed the Owl who flapped in front making the snowflakes swirl about. They soon found the cave entrance where Ewa had been left, but she was no longer there, just the flattened patch where she had laid.

Zak and Zoe called to her. "Bewaa, Bewaa!" They listened for a response as the wind whistled eerily around the rocks – was that a bleat? They listened again, and to everyone's surprise came forth a tiny high-pitched cry – it was coming from inside the cave. Farmer Jones sharply ordered the others to stay put, he fumbled into his deep jacket pocket, found his torch and slowly went into the cave.

Zak, Zoe, and Meg shivered impatiently at the entrance of the cave, Bobbin bobbed up again from nowhere to join them. Howell wobbled with tiredness on a nearby branch, blinking his big eyes open not to miss any developments. Meg sniffed the air to detect any clues but was relieved that her master hadn't called her into the darkness of the cave.

Zak and Zoe thought about their eventful time, how it all began on that twisted branch and if they hadn't got stuck there — would they have ever found Ewa? They were not to know that I, the Proper Dragon, had wished them there for that very special reason. Now we are nearing the conclusion of my proper dragon's tale and it is a time to remember that we may all need to believe in a dragon every now and again. One may be nearer than you think and strange matters can happen when you least expect it.

Then it was strangely noticed, the falling snow began to dwindle, a shaft of sunlight beamed through a cloud and shone onto the side of the mountain. The farmer appeared from the cave cradling the sweetest little red lamb. Ewa followed closely sniffing her new baby and feeling very pleased with herself. Zak and Zoe gasped with amazement at the unexpected sight and waggled their tails with delight. Meg licked the lamb's tiny feet — they tasted good and she woofed with excitement — Bobbin bolted away while Howell wearily uttered, "O good, now I can go to bed," and retired to his gap in the rocks.

That evening the snow began to dissolve leaving the mountains looking like iced buns in the moonlight. The wild weather had passed and the valley was peaceful again. The gentle trickle of the thawing snow made its way to the river while further up the valley the little Chapel stirred where the sound of organ music prompted the faithful few into devotional chorus.

In the cosy barn the flock were happily gossiping to each other, they were so glad to be reunited with the cheeky twins. Ewa proudly nursed her little lamb, he looked a healthy soul and was just like Sam the ram, while the others fussed about in their motherly way. Meg limped in with her leg in a bandage, she gently sniffed the new lamb then woofed goodnight to the sheep before returning to the farmhouse to sleep by the fire, a really special treat.

Howell the Owl flew into the barn after a good day's doze, Merlin the cat alertly swiped his paw towards him, intrigued by his fluttering. All the sheep baaed praise to Howell their hero. They invited him to stay for the winter in their wrinkly tin barn, but he insisted, "I'm no barn owl, I'm just a visitor."

Old farmer Jones crossed the mucky yard to the barn and for a peculiar moment thought he saw a dragon's print in the mud. He brought in a bucket of feed for Ewa and chuckled to himself — her new lamb had the reddest fleece he had ever seen. Soon everyone in the valley would hear of this amazing story.

Ewa named her lamb Bracken and when he matured into a fully, grown ram
he became the father of the new flock bringing back strong spirit and instinct
to the Black Mountain Sheep.

. . . . .there's lovely.

Proper Dragon Tales

If you have enjoyed this book, you may like to visit the website at www.properdragontales.co.uk to see the other books and products available in this series. To join the mailing list and be informed of new releases please use the "contact caroline" puff or email her at downey@properdragontales.co.uk. Caroline welcomes your comments or book reviews which can be submitted via the "book reviews" section of the website.

No.2 'Shadows in the Fforest' follows the capers of Larry long-legs the naughty lurcher-dog where he disrupts the peacefulness of the valley. But he has a plan to put things right and he ventures with Pickles the Trekking Pony into the woods where peculiar and wonderful events send them deeper into the forest.
Published Sept. 07

ISBN 978-0-9553618-1-4

No.3 'Secret of the Standing Stones' is revealed to Gwillim the greedy Billy Goat who suffers the consequences of eating a scrap too many - when scarecrow and canvas tent seemed to be his preferred feast. His adventure into the sacred circle of ancient rocks presents a challenging time for Gwillim.
Published Sept. 08

ISBN 978-0-9553618-2-1

Proper Dragon Tales

You may order directly from Caroline Downey or via the Website.
Framed Canvas Prints are available from images in this book.
Please quote titles and code numbers.

Prints are of high quality and produced on Canvas
with a gold-grained finished Frame
Image size 14x14ins. Framed size 18x18ins.
images will not have any borders or titles showing

Other products available in
this range include
Badges, Greetings Cards
and T-shirts.